Horror Stories

THE HOUND OF THE BASKERVILLES

Sir Arthur Conan Doyle

abridged edition

Mr Sherlock Holmes

Mr Sherlock Holmes, who was usually very late in the mornings, save when he stayed up all night, was seated at the breakfast table. I picked up the stick which our visitor had left behind him the night before. Just under the head was a broad silver band. 'To James Mortimer, M.R.C.S., from his friends of the C.C.H.', was engraved upon it.

"Well, Watson?"

"I think that Dr Mortimer is a successful elderly medical man. I think also that he is a country practitioner who does a great deal of his visiting on foot."

"Why so?"

"Because this stick has been so knocked about that I can hardly imagine a town practitioner carrying it. And then again, there is the 'friends of the C.C.H.'. I should guess that to be the Something Hunt."

"I am afraid that most of your conclusions were erroneous. Not that you are entirely wrong in this instance. The man is certainly a country practitioner. And he walks a great deal. I would suggest that a presentation to a doctor is likely to come from a hospital and that when the initials 'C.C.' are placed before that hospital the words 'Charing Cross' very naturally suggest themselves. On what occasion would it be most probable that such a presentation would be made? Obviously when Dr Mortimer withdrew from the hospital in order to start in practice for himself. So there emerges a young fellow under thirty, amiable, unambitious, absent-minded."

As we spoke, the doctor himself arrived.

"I am so very glad," said he, "I was not sure whether I had left it here. Glad to meet you, sir. You interest me very much, Mr Holmes. I had hardly expected so dolichocephalic a skull or such well-marked supra-orbital development. A cast of your skull, sir, until the original is available, would be an ornament to any anthropological museum."

"I presume, sir," said Holmes at last, "that it was not merely for the purpose of examining my skull that you have done me the honour to call here last night and again today?"

"No, sir. I came to you, Mr Holmes, because I am suddenly confronted with a most serious and extraordinary problem."

The Curse of the Baskervilles

"I have in my pocket a manuscript," said Dr James Mortimer. "This family paper was committed to my care by Sir Charles Baskerville, whose sudden and tragic death some three months ago created so much excitement in Devonshire. I was his personal friend as well as his medical attendant. He took this document very seriously."

Holmes stretched out his hand for the manuscript and flattened it upon his knee.

At the head was written: 'Baskerville Hall', and below, in large scrawling figures: '1742'.

Dr Mortimer read in a high, crackling voice the following curious, old-world narrative:

"Know that in the time of the Great Rebellion, this Manor of Baskerville was held by Hugo of that name, a most wild, profane, and godless man. Hugo came to love the daughter of a yeoman. One Michaelmas this Hugo, with five or six of his idle and wicked companions, stole down upon the farm and carried off the maiden. When they had brought her to the Hall the maiden was placed in an upper chamber. At last in the stress of her fear, by the aid of the growth of ivy which covered (and still covers) the south wall, she came down from under the eaves, and so homeward across the moor.

"It chanced that some little time later Hugo found the cage empty and the bird escaped. Then he cried aloud that he would that very night render his body and soul to the Powers of Evil if he might but overtake the wench. Hugo ran from the house, crying to his groom that they should saddle his mare and unkennel the pack, and giving the hounds a kerchief of the maid's he swung them to the line, and so off full cry in the moonlight over the moor.

"Everything was now in an uproar. But at length the drunken men started in pursuit.

"They had gone a mile or two when they passed one of the night shepherds upon the moorlands, and they cried to him to know if he had seen the hunt. And the man, as the story goes, was so crazed with fear that he could scarce speak, but at last he said that he had indeed seen the unhappy maiden, with the hounds upon her track. 'But I have seen more than that,' said he, 'for Hugo Baskerville passed me upon his black mare, and there ran mute beside him such a hound of hell as God forbid should ever be at my heels.'

"So the drunken squires cursed the shepherd and rode onwards. But soon their skins turned cold, for the black mare, dabbled with white froth, went past with trailing bridle and empty saddle. Riding slowly they came at last upon the hounds, whimpering in a cluster, some slinking away and some, with starting hackles and staring eyes, gazing down the narrow valley before them.

"There lay the unhappy maid where she had fallen, dead of fear and fatigue. But it was not the sight of her body, nor that of the body of Hugo Baskerville lying near her, which raised the hair upon the heads of these roisterers, but that, standing over Hugo, and plucking at his throat, there stood a foul thing, a great, black beast, shaped like a hound yet larger than any hound that ever mortal eye has rested upon. And as they looked the thing tore the throat out of Hugo Baskerville, on which, as it turned with blazing eyes and dripping jaws upon them, they shrieked with fear and rode for dear life, still screaming.

across the moor."

Dr Mortimer drew a folded newspaper from out of his pocket.

"Now, Mr Holmes, we will give you something a little more recent. This is the *Devon County Chronicle* of June 14th of this year.

"The recent sudden death of Sir Charles Baskerville has cast a gloom over the county. The facts of the case are simple. Sir Charles Baskerville was in the habit every night before going to bed of walking down the famous Yew Alley of Baskerville Hall. The evidence of his servants, Mr and Mrs Barrymore, shows that on the 4th of June Sir Charles went out as usual for his nocturnal walk, in the course of which he was in the habit of smoking a cigar. Half-way down this walk there is a gate which leads out on to the moor. There were indications that Sir Charles had stood for some little time here. He then proceeded down the Alley, and it was at the far end of it that his body was discovered. Barrymore states that his master's footprints altered their character from the time he passed the moor-gate, and that he appeared from thence onwards to have been walking upon his toes. The post-mortem examination showed long-standing organic disease, and the coroner's jury returned a verdict in accordance with the medical evidence. It is understood that the next-of-kin is Mr Henry Baskerville, the son of Sir Charles Baskerville's younger brother. The young man, when last heard of, was in America, and inquiries are being instituted with a view to informing him of his good fortune."

"This article contains all the public facts?"

"It does."

"Then let me have the private ones."

"The moor is very sparsely inhabited, and those who live near each other are thrown very much together. I saw a good deal of Sir Charles Baskerville. With the exception of Mr Frankland, of Lafter Hall, and Mr Stapleton, the naturalist, there are no other men of education within many miles.

"Within the last few months it became increasingly plain to me that Sir Charles's nervous system was strained to breaking-point. He had taken this legend exceedingly to heart.

"His heart was, I knew, affected, and the constant anxiety was evidently having a serious effect upon his health. Mr Stapleton, a mutual friend, was of the same opinion.

"On the night of Sir Charles's death, I saw the spot at the moor-gate where he seemed to have waited, I remarked the change in the shape of the prints after that point. There was certainly no physical injury of any kind. Barrymore said that there were no traces upon the ground round the body. He did not observe any. But I did – some little distance off, but fresh and clear."

Dr Mortimer looked strangely at us for an instant, and his voice sank almost to a whisper as he said: "Mr Holmes, they were the footprints of a gigantic hound!"

The Problem

I confess that at these words a shudder passed through me. Holmes leaned forward in his excitement.

"How was it that no one else saw it?"

"The marks were some twenty yards from the body, and no one gave them a thought. I don't suppose I should have done so had I not known this legend."

"But it had not approached the body?"

"No."

"What sort of night was it?"

"Damp and raw."

"What is the Alley like?"

"There are two lines of old yew hedge, twelve feet high and impenetrable. The walk in the centre is about eight feet across."

"I understand that the yew hedge is penetrated at one point by a gate?"

"Yes, the wicket-gate which leads on to the moor."

"So that to reach the Yew Alley one either has to come down it from the house or else to enter it by the moor-gate?"

"There is an exit through a summer-house at the far end; Sir Charles lay about fifty yards from it."

Sherlock Holmes struck his hand against his knee with an impatient gesture.

"If I had only been there!" he cried. "Now, how can I assist you?"

"By advising me as to what I should do with Sir Henry Baskerville."

"There is no other claimant, I presume?"

"None. The only other kinsman was Rodger Baskerville, the youngest of three brothers of whom poor Sir Charles was the elder. The second brother, who died young, is the father of this lad Henry. The third, Rodger, was the black sheep of the family. He fled to Central America, and died there in 1876 of yellow fever. Henry is the last of the Baskervilles. Now Mr Holmes, what would you advise me to do with him?"

"I recommend, sir, that you proceed to Waterloo to meet Sir Henry Baskerville. At ten o'clock tomorrow, Dr Mortimer, I will be much obliged to you if you will call upon me here, and bring Sir Henry Baskerville with you."

"I will do so, Mr Holmes."

"Thank you. Good morning."

"What do you make of it?" asked Holmes later.

"It is very bewildering."

"It has certainly a character of its own. There are points of distinction about it. That change in the footprints, for example. What do you make of that?"

"Mortimer said that the man had walked on tiptoe down that portion of the alley."

"He was running, Watson – running desperately, running for his life, running until he burst his heart and fell dead upon his face."

"Running from what?"

"There lies our problem."

Sir Henry Baskerville

The clock had just struck ten when Dr Mortimer was shown up, followed by the young baronet.

"This is Sir Henry Baskerville," said Dr Mortimer.

"Mr Holmes, if my friend here had not proposed coming round to you this morning I should have come on my own."

He laid an envelope upon the table, and we all bent over it. The address, 'Sir Henry Baskerville, Northumberland Hotel', was printed in rough characters; the post-mark 'Charing Cross' and the date of posting the preceding evening.

"Hum! Someone seems to be very deeply interested in your movements." Out of the envelope he took a half-sheet of paper. Across the middle of it a single sentence had been formed by pasting printed words upon it. It ran: "As you value your life or your reason keep away from the moor".

"Have you yesterday's *Times*, Watson?"

Holmes glanced over the paper, and deduced that the letters came from it.

"*The Times* is seldom found in any hands but those of the highly educated. Now, I am almost certain that this address has been written in an hotel."

"How can you say that?"

"If you examine it carefully you will see that both the pen and ink have given the writer trouble. Now, a private pen or ink-bottle is seldom allowed to be in such a state. But you know the hotel ink and the hotel pen, where it is rare to get anything else. I think we have drawn as much as we can from this curious letter; and now, Sir Henry, has anything else of interest happened to you since you have been in London?"

Sir Henry smiled. "I don't know much of British life yet, but I hope that to lose one of your boots is not part of the ordinary routine of life over here. I put them both outside my door last night, and there was only one in the morning. The worst of it is that I only bought the pair last night in the Strand, and I have never had them on."

"It seems a singularly useless thing to steal," said Holmes.

"And now, gentlemen," said the baronet, "it is time that you gave me a full account of what we are all driving at."

Dr Mortimer presented the whole case as he had done upon the morning before.

"The practical point which we now have to decide, Sir Henry, is whether it is or is not advisable for you to go to Baskerville Hall."

"There is no devil in hell, Mr Holmes, who can prevent me from going to the home of my own people, and you may take that to be my final answer. Now, it's half-past eleven, and I am going back right away to my hotel. Suppose you and your friend, Dr Watson, come round and lunch with us at two? I'll be able to tell you more clearly then how this thing strikes me."

We heard the steps of our visitors descend the stair and the bang of the front door. In an instant Holmes became the man of action.

"Your hat and boots, Watson, quick! Not a moment to lose!" We hurried together down the stairs and into the street. Then we followed into Oxford Street and so down Regent Street. An instant afterwards he gave a little cry of satisfaction, and I saw that a hansom cab with a man inside which had halted on the other side of the street was now walking slowly onwards again.

"There's our man, Watson!"

At that instant I was aware of a bushy black beard and a pair of piercing eyes turned upon us through the side window of the cab. Instantly the

trapdoor at the top flew up, something was screamed to the driver, and the cab flew madly off down Regent Street. Holmes looked eagerly round for another, but no empty one was in sight.

"There now!" said Holmes, bitterly. "Could you swear to that man's face within the cab?"

"I could swear only to the beard."

"And so could I – from which I gather that in all probability it was a false one. Come in here, Watson!"

He turned into one of the district messenger offices, where he was warmly greeted by the manager.

A lad of fourteen, with a bright, keen face, obeyed the summons of the manager.

"Now, there are the names of twenty-three hotels here, all in the immediate neighbourhood of Charing Cross. You will visit each of these in turn. You are looking for yesterday's *Times* with some holes cut in it with scissors. Let me have a report by wire at Baker Street before evening. And now, Watson, it only remains for us to find out by wire the identity of the cabman, No 2704."

Three Broken Threads

Soon, we found ourselves at the Northumberland Hotel.

"Sir Henry Baskerville is upstairs expecting you," said the clerk.

As we came round the top of the stairs we ran up

against Sir Henry Baskerville himself. His face was flushed with anger, and he held an old and dusty boot in one of his hands.

"Seems to me they are playing me for a sucker in this hotel," he cried. "They'll find they've started in to monkey with the wrong man unless they are careful.. By thunder, if that chap can't find my missing boot there will be trouble."

"Still looking for your boot?"

"Yes, sir, and mean to find it."

"But surely, you said that it was a new brown boot?"

"So it was, sir. And now it's an old black one."

"What! you don't mean to say –?"

"That's just what I do mean to say. I only had three pairs in the world – the new brown, the old black, and the patent leathers, which I am wearing. Last night they took one of my brown ones, and today they have sneaked one of the black."

It was in the private sitting-room to which we afterwards repaired that Holmes asked Baskerville what were his intentions.

"To go to Baskerville Hall."

"On the whole," said Holmes, "I think that your decision is a wise one. Dr Mortimer, have you among your neighbours or acquaintances on Dartmoor any man with a black, full beard?"

"No – or, let me see – why yes. Barrymore, Sir Charles's butler, is a man with a full, black beard."

"Who is this Barrymore?" asked Baskerville.

"He is the son of the old caretaker, who is dead. They have looked after the Hall for four generations now. So far as I know, he and his wife are as respectable a couple as any in the county."

"Quite so. Well, Sir Henry, I am of one mind with you as to the advisability of your going down to Devonshire without delay. There is only one provision which I must make. You certainly must not go alone."

"Is it possible that you could come yourself, Mr Holmes?"

"At the present instant one of the most revered names in England is being besmirched by a blackmailer, and only I can stop a disastrous scandal. You will see how impossible it is for me to go to Dartmoor."

"Whom would you recommend to accompany me, then?"

Holmes laid his hand upon my arm.

"If my friend would undertake it there is no man who is better worth having at your side when you are in a tight place."

"I will come with pleasure," said I.

"Then on Saturday, unless you hear to the contrary, we shall meet at the 10.30 train from Paddington."

We had risen to depart when Baskerville gave a cry of triumph, and driving into one of the corners of the room he drew a brown boot from under a cabinet.

"My missing boot!" he cried.

"May all our difficulties vanish as easily!" said

Sherlock Holmes.

Just before dinner a telegram was handed in. It ran: Visited twenty-three hotels as directed, but sorry to report unable to trace cut sheet of *Times*.

"We have still the cabman who drove the spy."

"Exactly. I should not be surprised if this were an answer to my question."

The ring at the bell proved to be the cab-driver himself.

"First of all your name and address."

"John Clayton, 3, Turpey Street, the Borough."

"Now, Clayton, tell me all about the fare who came and watched this house at ten o'clock this morning and afterwards followed the two gentlemen down Regent Street."

"The gentleman told me that he was a detective, and that I was to say nothing about him to anyone."

"When did he say this?"

"When he left me."

"Did he say anything more?"

"He mentioned his name."

"Oh, he mentioned his name, did he? What was the name that he mentioned?"

"His name," said the cabman, "was Mr Sherlock Holmes."

Baskerville Hall

Sir Henry Baskerville and Dr Mortimer were

ready upon the appointed day, and we started as arranged for Devonshire. Holmes gave me his last parting injunction and advice.

"I wish you simply to report facts in the fullest possible manner to me, and leave me to do the theorizing."

"I will do my best."

"Keep you revolver near you night and day, and never relax your precautions."

The journey was a swift and pleasant one.

The train pulled up at a small wayside station, and we all descended. Outside, a wagonette with a pair of cobs was waiting. The coachman saluted Sir Henry, and in a few minutes we were flying swiftly down the broad white road.

A steep curve of heath-clad land lay in front of us. On the summit was a mounted soldier, dark and stern, his rifle poised ready over his forearm.

Our driver half turned in his seat.

"There's a convict escaped from Princetown, sir. He's been out three days now, but no sight of him yet. The farmers about here don't like it, sir, and that's a fact."

"Who is he, then?"

"It is Selden, the Notting Hill murderer."

Suddenly we looked down into a cup-like depression, patched with stunted oaks and firs which had been twisted and bent by the fury of years of storm. Two high, narrow towers rose over the trees. The driver pointed with his whip.

"Baskerville Hall," said he.

A tall man stepped from the shadow of the

porch to open the door of the wagonette. The figure of a woman was silhouetted against the yellow light of the hall.

Barrymore was a remarkable-looking man, tall, handsome, with a square black beard and pale distinguished features.

On retiring to bed, I found myself weary and yet wakeful, tossing restlessly from side to side. And then suddenly, in the very dead of the night, there came a sound to my ears, clear, resonant, and unmistakable. It was the sob of a woman, the muffled, strangling gasp of one who is torn by an uncontrollable sorrow.

The Stapletons of Merripit House

"Did you happen to hear a woman sobbing in the night?" I asked the baronet next morning.

"I did." He rang the bell and asked Barrymore whether he could account for our experience. It seemed to me that the pallid features of the butler turned a shade paler.

"There are only two women in the house, Sir Henry," he answered. "One is the scullery-maid, who sleeps in the other wing. The other is my wife, and the sound could not have come from her."

And yet he lied as he said it, for it chanced that I met Mrs Barrymore in the long corridor with the sun full upon her face. Her tell-tale eyes were red and glanced at me from between swollen lids. It was she, then, who wept in the night, and if she

did so her husband must know it. Yet he had taken the obvious risk of discovery in declaring that it was not so. Why had he done this? And why did she weep so bitterly? Was it possible that it had been Barrymore whom we had seen in the cab in Regent Street?

I took a pleasant walk of four miles along the edge of the moor, leading me at last to a small grey hamlet.

Suddenly my thoughts were interrupted by the sound of running feet behind me and by a voice which called me by name. It was a stranger who was pursuing me. He was a small, slim, clean-shaven man, flaxen-haired, between thirty and forty years of age. A tin box for botanical specimens hung over his shoulder, and he carried a green butterfly-net.

"You will, I am sure, excuse my presumption, Dr Watson," said he, as he came panting up to where I stood. "Here on the moor we are homely folk, and do not wait for formal introductions. I am Stapleton, of Merripit House. I have been calling on Mortimer, and he pointed you out to me. I trust that Sir Henry is none the worse for his journey?"

"He is very well, thank you."

"Of course you know the legend of the fiend dog which haunts the family? The story took a great hold upon Sir Charles, and I feared that some disaster might occur."

"You think then, that some dog pursued Sir Charles, and that he died of fright in consequence?"

"Have you any better explanation?"

"I have not come to any conclusion."

"Has Mr Sherlock Holmes?"

The words took away my breath for an instant, but a glance at the placid face and steadfast eyes of my companion showed no surprise was intended.

"It is useless for us to pretend that we do not know you, Dr Watson," said he. "The records of your detective have reached us here. If you are here, then it follows that Mr Sherlock Holmes is interesting himself in the matter, and I am naturally curious to know what view he may take."

"I am afraid that I cannot answer that question."

"You are perfectly right to be wary and discreet. A moderate walk along this moor-path brings us to Merripit House," said he. "Perhaps you will spare an hour that I may have the pleasure of introducing you to my sister."

I accepted Stapleton's invitation, and we turned together down the path.

"It is a wonderful place, the moor," said he. "You notice those bright green spots scattered thickly over it?"

"Yes, they seem more fertile than the rest."

Stapleton laughed. "That is the great Grimpen Mire. A false step yonder means death to man or beast."

"What is that?"

A long, low moan, indescribably sad, swept over the moor. From a dull murmur it swelled into a deep roar and then sank back into a melancholy, throbbing murmur once again. Stapleton looked at me with a curious expression on his face.

"The peasants say it is the Hound of the Baskervilles calling for its prey. I've heard it once or twice before, but never quite so loud."

"You are an educated man. You don't believe such nonsense as that?" said I. "What do you think is the cause of so strange a sound?"

"Bogs make queer noises sometimes. It's the mud settling, or the water rising, or something."

A small moth fluttered across our path, and in an instant Stapleton was rushing in pursuit of it. I was watching his pursuit, when I found a woman near me upon the path.

I could not doubt that this was the Miss Stapleton of whom I had been told. There could not have been a greater contrast between brother and sister, for Stapleton was neutral-tinted, with light hair and grey eyes, while she was darker than any brunette whom I have seen in England – slim, elegant, and tall. She had a proud, finely cut face, a sensitive mouth and beautiful dark, eager eyes.

"Go back!" she said. "Go straight back to London, instantly."

"Why should I go back?" I asked.

"I cannot explain. But for God's sake do what I ask you. Go back to London! Hush, my brother is coming!"

Stapleton had abandoned the chase, and came back to us breathing hard and flushed with his exertions.

"Halloa, Beryl!" said he.

"Well, Jack, you are very hot."

"You have introduced yourselves, I can see."

"I was telling Sir Henry that it was rather late for him to see the true beauties of the moor."

"Why, who do you imagine this is?"

"Sir Henry Baskerville."

"No, no," said I. "My name is Dr Watson."

"We have been talking at cross purposes," said she. "But you will come on, will you not, and see Merripit House?"

A short walk brought us to it, a bleak moorland house, once the farm of some grazier in the old prosperous days, but now put into repair and turned into a modern dwelling.

"Queer spot to choose, is it not?" said he, as if in answer to my thought. "And yet we manage to make ourselves fairly happy, do we not, Beryl?"

"Quite happy," said she, but there was no ring of conviction in her words.

"I had a school," said Stapleton. "It was in the North Country. A serious epidemic broke out in the school, and three of the boys died. It never recovered from the blow, and much of my capital was irretrievably swallowed up. We have books, we have our studies, and we have interesting neighbours. Poor Sir Charles was an admirable companion."

I was eager to get back to my charge. I resisted

all pressure to stay for lunch, and I set off at once upon my return journey, taking the grass-grown path by which we had come.

First Report of Dr Watson

Baskerville Hall, Oct. 13th

My Dear Holmes,

I must keep you in touch with some of the factors in the situation.

One of these is the escaped convict upon the moor. A fortnight has passed since his flight, during which he has not been seen and nothing has been heard of him. Of course so far as his concealment goes there is no difficulty at all. Any

one of these stone huts would give him a hiding-place.

I confess that I have had uneasy moments when I have thought of the Stapletons. Both Sir Henry and I were concerned at their situation, and it was suggested that Perkins, the groom, should go over to sleep there, but Stapleton would not hear of it.

The fact is that our friend the baronet begins to display a considerable interst in our fair neighbour.

Stapleton came over to call upon Baskerville on that first day, and the very next morning he took us both to show us the spot where the legend of the wicked Hugo is supposed to have had its origin.

On our way back we stayed for lunch at Merripit House, and it was there that Sir Henry made the acquaintance of Miss Stapleton. From the first moment he appeared to be strongly attracted and I am much mistaken if the feeling was not mutual. Stapleton seems to dislike Sir Henry paying attention to his sister.

One other neighbour I have met is Mr Frankland, of Lafter Hall. He is an elderly man, red-faced, white-haired, and choleric. His passion is for the British law, and he has spent a large fortune in litigation. Being an amateur astonomer, he has an excellent telescope, with which he lies upon the roof of his own house and sweeps the moor all day in the hope of catching a glimpse of the escaped convict.

And now, having brought you up to date, let me end on that which is most important and tell you more about the Barrymores, and especially about the surprising developments of last night.

Last night, about two in the morning, I was aroused by a stealthy step passing my room. It was Barrymore. I followed him. I could see from the glimmer of light through an open door that he had entered one of the rooms. I peeped round the corner of the door.

Barrymore was crouching at the window with the candle held against the glass. His face seemed to be rigid with expectation as he stared out into the blackness of the moor. I have had a long talk with Sir Henry this morning, and we have made a plan of campaign founded upon my observations of last night.

The Light Upon the Moor

Baskerville Hall, Oct. 15th

My Dear Holmes,

Before breakfast I examined the room in which Barrymore had been on the night before. It commands the nearest outlook on to the moor. It follows, therefore, that Barrymore must have been looking out for something or somebody upon the moor. The night was very dark, so that I can hardly imagine how he could have hoped to see anyone.

I had an interview with the baronet in his study after breakfast, and I told him all that I had seen.

"I knew that Barrymore walked about nights,

and I had a mind to speak to him about it," said he.

"We'll sit up tonight, and wait until he passes."

Sir Henry put on his hat and prepared to go out. As a matter of course, I did the same.

"What, are *you* coming, Watson?" he asked.

"Well, you know what my instructions are. Holmes insisted that I should not leave you, and especially that you should not go alone upon the moor."

Sir Henry put his hand upon my shoulder with a pleasant smile.

"My dear fellow," said he, "Holmes, with all his wisdom, did not foresee some things which have happened since I have been on the moor. You understand me? I must go out alone."

I decided that I must follow him, so I set off at once in the direction of Merripit House.

I hurried along the road at the top of my speed without seeing anything of Sir Henry, until I came to the point where the moor path branches off. Then I saw him at once. He was on the moor path, about a quarter of a mile off, and a lady was by his side who could only be Miss Stapleton.

I was suddenly aware that I was not the only witness of their interview. Stapleton was very much closer to the pair than I was, and he appeared to be moving in their direction. At this instant Sir Henry suddenly drew Miss Stapleton to his side. Next moment I saw them sprint apart and turn hurriedly round. Stapleton was running wildly towards them. He gesticulated and almost danced with excitement in front of the lovers. Finally Stapleton turned upon his heel and beckoned in a peremptory way to his sister, who, after an irresolute glance at Sir Henry, walked off by the side of her brother.

What all this meant I could not imagine, but I was deeply ashamed to have witnessed so intimate a scene without my friend's knowledge. I ran down the hill, therefore, and met the baronet at the bottom. His face was flushed with anger.

"Did he ever strike you as being crazy – this brother of hers?" he asked me.

"I can't say that he ever did."

"I dare say not. I always thought him sane enough until today, but you can take it from me that either he or I ought to be in a strait-jacket. What's the matter with me, anyhow? Is there anything that would prevent me from making a good husband to a woman that I loved?"

"I should say not."

"He can't object to my worldly position, so it must be myself that he has this down on. What has he against me? He was just white with rage, and those light eyes of his were blazing with fury. What was I doing with the lady? How dared I offer her attentions which were distasteful to her? As it was I told him that my feelings towards his sister were such as I was not ashamed of, and that I hoped that she might honour me by becoming my wife. That seemed to make the matter no better, so than I lost my temper too. So it ended by his going off with her, as you saw."

I was completely puzzled myself. However, our conjectures were set at rest by a visit from Stapleton himself that very afternoon. He had come to offer apologies for his rudeness of the morning, and after a long private interview with Sir Henry in his study the upshot of their conversation was that the breach is quite healed, and that we are to dine at Merripit House next Friday as a sign of it.

And now I pass on to another thread which I have extricated out of the tangled skein, the mystery of the sobs in the night, of the tear-stained face of Mrs Barrymore, and of the secret journeys of the butler to the western lattice-window.

I sat up with Sir Henry in his room until nearly three o'clock in the morning, and we had almost given it up in despair, when we heard the creak of a step in the passage. Then we set out in pursuit. When at last we reached the door and peeped through we found him crouching at the window, candle in hand, his white, intent face pressed against the pane.

The baronet walked into the room, and as he did so, Barrymore sprang up from the window with a sharp hiss of his breath.

"Look here, Barrymore," said Sir Henry, sternly, "we have made up our minds to have the truth out of you. Come, now! No lies! What were you doing at that window?"

"Don't ask me, Sir Henry – don't ask me!"

"He must have been holding the candle as a

signal," said I.

I held it as he had done, and stared out into the darkness of the night. And then a tiny pinpoint of yellow light glowed steadily in the centre of the window.

"I will not tell."

"By thunder, you may well be ashamed of yourself. Your family has lived with mine for over a hundred years under this roof, and here I find you deep in some dark plot against me."

"No, no, sir; not against you!"

It was a woman's voice, and Mrs Barrymore was standing at the door.

"It is my doing, Sir Henry – all mine. My unhappy brother is starving on the moor. The light is a signal to him that food is ready for him, and his light out yonder is to show the spot to which to bring it."

"Then your brother is –"

"The escaped convict, sir – Selden, the criminal."

"Is this true, Barrymore?"

"Yes, Sir Henry."

"Well, I cannot blame you for standing by your own wife. Go to your room, you two, and we shall talk further about this matter in the morning."

When they were gone we looked out of the window again. Far away in the black distance there still glowed that one tiny point of yellow light.

"By thunder, Watson, I am going out to take that man!"

"I will come," said I.

"Then get your revolver and put on your boots."

"I say, Watson," said the baronet, "what would Holmes say to this? How about that hour of darkness in which the power of evil is exalted?"

We stumbled slowly along in the darkness, with the yellow speck of light burning steadily in front. A guttering candle was stuck in a crevice.

"What shall we do now?"

"Wait here. Let us see if we can get a glimpse of him."

The words were hardly out of my mouth when we both saw him. I sprang forward, and Sir Henry did the same. At the same moment the convict sprang to his feet and turned to run.

We saw him for a long time in the moonlight, until he was only a small speck. Finally we stopped and sat panting on two rocks.

The moon was low and the jagged pinnacle of a granite tor stood up against the lower curve of its silver disc. There outlined I saw the figure of a man upon the tor, a tall, thin man. He stood with his legs a little separated, his arms folded, his head bowed. It was not the convict. With a cry of surprise I pointed him out to the baronet, but the man was gone.

Extract from Dr Watson's Diary

October 16th – We had a small scene this morning after breakfast. Barrymore asked leave to speak with Sir Henry, and they were closeted in his study some little time. After a time the baronet opened his door and called for me.

"Barrymore thinks that is was unfair on our part to hunt his brother-in-law down when he, of his own free will, had told us the secret."

"The man is a public danger. There are lonely houses scattered over the moor, and he is a fellow who would stick at nothing. There's no safety for anyone until he is under lock and key."

"I assure you, Sir Henry, that in a very few days he will be on his way to South Africa. For God's sake, sir, I beg of you not to let the police know that he is still on the moor."

"I guess we are aiding and abetting a felony, Watson? All right, Barrymore, you can go."

With a few broken words of gratitude the man turned, but he hesitated and then came back.

"You've been so kind to us, sir. I know something, Sir Henry, about poor Sir Charles's death."

"What, then?"

"I know why he was at the gate at that hour. It was to meet a woman. I can't give you the name, sir, but I can give you the initials. Her initials were L.L. Sir Henry, your uncle had a letter that morning. It was from Coombe Tracey, and it was addressed in a woman's hand. Only a few weeks ago my wife was cleaning out Sir Charles's study and she found the ashes of a burned letter in the back of the grate. The greater part of it was charred to pieces, but one little slip, the end of a page, hung together. It seemed to us to be a postscript and it said: 'Please, please, as you are a gentleman, burn this letter, and be at the gate by ten o'clock.' Beneath it were signed the initials L.L."

"And you have no idea who L.L. is?"

"No, sir."

I went at once to my room and drew up my report for Holmes. It was evident to me that he had been very busy of late, for the notes which I had from Baker Street were few and short, with no comments upon the information which I had supplied, and hardly any reference to my mission. I wish that he were here.

October 17th – In the evening I walked far upon the sodden moor.

As I walked back I was overtaken by Dr Mortimer in his dog-cart. He gave me a lift homewards.

"By the way, Mortimer," said I, "I suppose there are few people living within driving distance whom you do not know?"

"Hardly any, I think."

"Can you, then, tell me the name of any woman whose initials are L.L.?"

"There is Laura Lyons – her initials are L.L. – she lives in Coombe Tracey. She is Frankland's daughter. She married an artist named Lyons, who proved to be a blackguard and deserted her. I fancy old Frankland allows her a pittance, but it cannot be more. Her story got about, and several of the people here did something to enable her to earn an honest living. Stapleton did for one, and Sir Charles for another. I gave a trifle myself. It was to set her up in a typewriting business."

The Man on the Tor

At breakfast, I informed the baronet about Laura Lyons, and it seemed to both of us that if I went alone the results might be better.

When I reached Coombe Tracey I had no difficulty in finding her rooms. A maid showed me in and as I entered the sitting-room a lady sprang up with a pleasant smile of welcome. Her face fell, when she saw that I was a stranger, and she asked me the object of my visit.

"It was about the late Sir Charles Baskerville that I have come here to see you. You knew him, did you not?"

"I owe a great deal to his kindness."

"Did you ever write to Sir Charles asking him to meet you?"

"Really, sir, this is a very extraordinary question."

"I am sorry, madam, but I must repeat it."

"Then I answer – certainly not."

"Not on the very day of Sir Charles's death?"

The flush had faded in an instant, and a deathly face was before me. Her dry lips could not speak the 'No' which I saw rather than heard.

"Surely your memory deceives you," said I. "I could even quote a passage of your letter. It ran

'Please, please, as you are a gentleman burn this letter, and be at the gate by ten o'clock'."

"Why should I deny it? I have no reason to be ashamed of it. I wished him to help me. I believed that if I had an interview I could gain his help, so I asked him to meet me."

"Well, what happened when you did get there?"

"I never went. Something intervened to prevent my going. I received help in the interval from another source."

"Why, then, did you not write to Sir Charles and explain this?"

"So I should have done had I not seen his death in the paper next morning."

Luck had been against us again and again in this inquiry, but now at last it came to my aid.

And the messenger of good fortune was none other than Mr Frankland.

"It is a great day for me, sir – one of the red-letter days of my life," he cried, with many chuckles.

"Some poaching case, no doubt?"

"Ha, ha, my boy, a very much more important matter than that! What about the convict on the moor?"

"How do you know that he is anywhere upon the moor?"

"I see him every day through my telescope upon the roof."

"I should say that it was much more likely that it was one of the moorland shepherds."

"Indeed, sir!" said he. "Do you see Black Tor over yonder? It is the stoniest part of the whole moor. Is that a place where a shepherd would be likely to take his station? Your suggestion, sir, is a most absurd one."

As soon as I could, I left his house, and then struck off across the moor and made for the stony hill.

The sun was already sinking when I reached the summit of the hill. Down beneath me was a circle of old stone huts, and in the middle of them there was one which retained sufficient roof to act as a screen against the weather. This must be the burrow where the stranger lurked.

As I approached the hut, I closed my hand upon the butt of my revolver, and walking swiftly up to the door, I looked in. The place was empty.

But there were ample signs that I had not come upon a false scent. A litter of empty tins showed that the place had been occupied for some time, and I saw a pannikin and a half-full bottle of spirits standing in the corner.

With tingling nerves, but a fixed purpose, I sat in the hut and waited for the coming of its tenant.

And then at last I heard him. I shrank back into the darkest corner, and cocked the pistol in my pocket. There was a long pause, which showed that he had stopped. Then once more the footsteps approached and a shadow fell across the opening of the hut.

"It is a lovely evening, my dear Watson," said a well-known voice. "I really think that you will be more comfortable outside than in."

Death on the Moor

For a moment or two I sat breathless, hardly able to believe my ears. That cold, incisive, ironical voice could belong to but one man in all the world.

"Holmes!" I cried. "Holmes!"

"Come out," said he, "and please be careful with the revolver."

"I never was more glad to see anyone in my life," said I.

"Or more astonished, eh?"

"Well, I must confess to it."

"So you have been to Coombe Tracey, have you? To see Mrs Laura Lyons?"

"Exactly."

I told Holmes of my conversation with the lady.

"This is most important," said he. "You are aware, perhaps, that a close intimacy exists between this lady and the man Stapleton?"

"I did not."

"There can be no doubt about the matter. Now, this puts a very powerful weapon into our hands. If I could only use it to detach his wife –"

"His wife?"

"The lady who has passed here as Miss Stapleton is in reality his wife."

"But why this elaborate deception?"

"Because he foresaw that she would be very much more useful to him in the character of a free woman."

"It is he, then, who is our enemy – it is he who dogged us in London? And the warning – it must have come from her!"

"Exactly."

"But are you sure of this, Holmes? How do you know that the woman is his wife?"

"Because he so far forgot himself as to tell you a true piece of autobiography upon the occasion when he first met you, and I dare say he has many a time regretted it since. He *was* once a schoolmaster in the North of England. A little investigation showed me that a school had come to grief under atrocious circumstances, and that the man who had owned it – the name was different – had disappeared with his wife. The description agreed."

45

"If this woman is in truth his wife, where does Mrs Laura Lyons come in?" I asked.

"Your interview with the lady has cleared the situation very much. I did not know about a projected divorce between herself and her husband. In that case, regarding Stapleton as an unmarried man, she counted no doubt upon becoming his wife."

"One last question, Holmes," I said, as I rose. "What is the meaning of it all? What is he after?"

"It is murder, Watson – refined, cold-blooded, deliberate murder. There is but one danger which can threaten us. It is that he should strike before we are ready to do so. Hark!"

A terrible scream – a prolonged yell of horror and anguish burst out of the silence of the moor.

Holmes had sprung to his feet.

Again the cry swept through the silent night, and a new sound mingled with it, a deep, muttered rumble, musical and yet menacing, rising and falling like the low, constant murmur of the sea.

"The hound!" cried Holmes.

Blindly we ran through the gloom, heading always in the direction whence those dreadful sounds had come. There was a sheer cliff, which overlooked a stone-strewn slope. On its jagged face was spreadeagled a prostrate man face downwards upon the ground, the head doubled under him at a horrible angle, the shoulders rounded and the body hunched together – the body of Selden, the criminal.

Then I remembered how the baronet had told me that he had handed his old wardrobe to Barrymore. Barrymore had passed it on in order to help Selden in his escape.

"It is clear enough that the hound has been laid on from some article of Sir Henry's – the boot which was abstracted in the hotel, in all probability – and so ran this man down."

"A great mystery to me is why this hound should be loose tonight. Stapleton would not let it go unless he had reason to think that Sir Henry would be there."

"Exactly. Halloa, Watson, what's this? It's the man himself, by all that's wonderful and audacious! Not a word or my plans crumble to the ground."

"Why, Dr Watson, what's this? Somebody hurt? Not – don't tell me that is our friend Sir Henry!"

He stooped over the dead man. I heard a sharp intake of his breath and the cigar fell from his fingers.

"Who – who's this?"

"It is Selden, the man who escaped from Princetown."

Stapleton turned a ghastly face upon us, but by a supreme effort he had overcome his amazement and his disappointment.

"Dear me! What a very shocking affair! How did he die?"

"He appears to have broken his neck by falling over these rocks. My friend and I were strolling on the moor when we heard a cry. I have no doubt that anxiety and exposure have driven him off his head. He has rushed about in a crazy state and eventually fallen over here and broken his neck."

"That seems the most reasonable theory," said Stapleton. "What do you think about it, Mr Sherlock Holmes?"

My friend bowed his compliments.

"You are quick at identification," said he.

"We have been expecting you in these parts since Dr Watson came down. You are in time to see a tragedy."

"Yes, indeed. I will take an unpleasant remembrance back to London with me tomorrow."

"Oh, you return tomorrow?"

"That is my intention."

Stapleton turned to me.

"I would suggest carrying this poor fellow to my house, but it would give my sister such a fright. I think that he will be safe until morning."

Holmes and I set off to Baskerville Hall, leaving the naturalist to return alone.

"We're at close grips at last," said Holmes. "I have great hopes of Mrs Laura Lyons. But one last word, Watson. Say nothing of the hound to Sir Henry. He will have a better nerve for the ordeal which he will have to undergo tomorrow."

Fixing the Nets

Sir Henry was more pleased than surprised to see

Sherlock Holmes, for he had for some days been expecting that recent events would bring him down from London.

"But how about the case?" asked the baronet. "Have you made anything out of the tangle?"

"I think I will muzzle the hound all right if you will give me your help. I will ask you also to do it blindly, without always asking the reason."

"Just as you like."

"If you will do this I have no doubt –"

He stopped suddenly and stared fixedly up over my head into the air.

"What is it?"

"These are all family portraits, I presume? Who is this Cavalier opposite to me – the one with the black velvet and the lace?"

"That is the cause of all the mischief, the wicked Hugo, who started the tale of the Hound of the Baskervilles."

It was not until later, when Sir Henry had gone to his room, that I was able to follow the trend of Holmes's thoughts. He led me back into the banqueting-hall, his bedroom candle in his hand, and he held it up against the time-stained portrait on the wall.

"Is it like anyone you know?"

"There is something of Sir Henry about the jaw."

"Just a suggestion, perhaps. But wait an instant!"

He stood upon a chair, and curved his right arm over the broad hat, and round the long ringlets.

"Good heavens!"

The face of Stapleton had sprung out of the canvas.

"Ha, you see it now. The fellow is a Baskerville – that is evident."

"With designs upon the succession."

"Exactly. We have him, Watson, we have him."

"Good morning, Holmes," said the baronet the next day. "You look like a general who is planning a battle with his chief of staff."

"That is the exact situation. Watson was asking for orders."

"And so do I."

"Very good. You are engaged, as I understand, to dine with our friends the Stapletons tonight. Watson and I must go to London. You can tell your friends that urgent business required us to be in town. Will you remember to give them that message?"

"If you insist upon it."

"We will drive in to Coombe Tracey, but Watson will leave his things as a pledge that he will come back to you. One more direction! I wish you to drive to Merripit House. Send back your trap, however, and let them know that you intend to walk home."

"To walk across the moor?"

"Yes. And as you value your life, do not go across the moor in any direction save along the straight path which leads from Merripit House to the Grimpen Road, and is your natural way home."

"I will do just what you say."

We bade goodbye and a couple of hours afterwards were at the station at Coombe Tracey. A small boy was waiting upon the platform.

"Any orders, sir?"

"Yes, ask at the station office if there is a message for me."

The boy returned with a telegram. It ran: Coming down with unsigned warrant. Arrive five-forty – LESTRADE.

"Now, Watson, I think that we cannot employ our time better than by calling upon your acquaintance, Mrs Laura Lyons."

Mrs Laura Lyons was in her office.

"I am investigating the death of the late Sir Charles Baskerville," said he. "I wish to be perfectly frank with you, Mrs Lyons. We regard this case as one of murder, and the evidence may implicate not only your friend, Mr Stapleton, but his wife as well."

"His wife!" she cried.

"The person who has passed for his sister is really his wife."

"Prove it to me! Prove it to me! And if you can do so –!" The fierce flash of her eyes said more than any words.

"Here is a photograph of the couple taken in York four years ago. It is endorsed 'Mr and Mrs Vandeleur', but you will have no difficulty in recognizing him, and her also, if you know her by sight."

"Mr Holmes," she said, "this man had offered me marriage on condition that I could get a divorce from my husband. He has lied to me, the villain, in every conceivable way. Ask me what you like, and there is nothing which I shall hold back. One thing I swear to you, and that is that when I wrote the letter I never dreamed of any harm to the old gentleman, who had been my kindest friend."

"I entirely believe you, madam," said Sherlock Holmes. "The sending of this letter was suggested to you by Stapleton?"

"Exactly."

"And then after you had sent the letter he dissuaded you from keeping the appointment?"

"He told me that it would hurt his self-respect."

"But you had your suspicions?"

"I knew him," she said. "But if he had kept faith with me I should always have done so with him."

"Our case becomes rounded off, and difficulty after difficulty thins away in front of us," said Holmes as we stood waiting for the arrival of the express from town.

The London express came roaring in and a small, wiry bulldog of a man sprung from a first-class carriage. We all three shook hands.

"Anything good?" asked Lestrade.

"The biggest thing for years," said Holmes.

The Hound of the Baskervilles

Later that night, we started to walk to Merripit House.

"Are you armed, Lestrade?"

The little detective smiled.

"Good! My friend and I are also ready for emergencies."

"You're mighty close about this affair, Mr Holmes. What's the game now?"

"A waiting game."

"My word, it does not seem a very cheerful place," said the detective. "I see the lights of a house ahead of us."

"That is Merripit House and the end of our journey. I must request you to walk on tiptoe and not to talk above a whisper."

Holmes halted us when we were about two hundred yards from it.

I tiptoed down the path and reached a point whence I could look straight through the uncurtained window.

There were only two men in the room, Sir Henry and Stapleton. Stapleton was talking with animation, but the baronet looked pale and distrait.

As I watched them Stapleton rose and left the room. I heard the creak of a door and the crisp sound of boots upon gravel. The steps passed along the path on the other side of the wall under which I crouched. I saw the naturalist pause at the door of an out-house in the corner of the orchard. A key turned in a lock, and as he passed in there was a curious scuffling noise from within. He was only a minute or so inside, and then I heard the key turn once more, and he passed me and re-entered the house.

"You say, Watson, that the lady is not there?" Holmes asked, when I had finished my report.

"No."

Holmes stamped his feet in his impatience.

A sound of quick steps broke the silence of the moor. The steps grew louder, and there stepped the baronet.

"Hist!" cried Holmes, and I heard the sharp click of a cocking pistol. "Look out! It's coming!"

There was a thin, crisp continuous patter. Holmes's eyes suddenly started forward in a rigid, fixed stare, and his lips parted in amazement. I sprang to my feet, my mind paralysed by the dreadful shape which had sprung out upon us from the shadows. A hound it was, an enormous coal-black hound, but not such a hound as mortal eyes have ever seen. Fire burst from its open mouth, its eyes glowed with a smouldering glare, its muzzle and hackles and dewlap were outlined in flickering flame.

Holmes and I both fired together, and the creature gave a hideous howl, which showed that one at least had hit him. He did not pause, however, but bounded onwards. Far away on the path we saw Sir Henry looking back, his face white in the moonlight, his hands raised in

horror, glaring helplessly at the frightful thing which was hunting him down.

Never have I seen a man run as Holmes ran that night. In front of us we heard scream after scream from Sir Henry and the deep roar of the hound. I was in time to see the beast spring upon its victim, hurl him to the ground and worry at his throat. But the next instant Holmes had emptied five barrels of his revolver into the creature's flank. The giant hound was dead.

Sir Henry lay insensible where he had fallen. We tore away his collar, and Holmes breathed a prayer of gratitude when we saw that there was no sign of a wound.

In mere size and strength it was a terrible creature which was lying stretched before us – gaunt, savage, and as large as a small lioness. Even now, in the stillness of death, the huge jaws seemed to be dripping with a bluish flame, and the small, deep-set, cruel eyes were ringed with fire. I placed my hand upon the glowing muzzle, and as I held them up my own fingers smouldered and gleamed in the darkness.

"Phosphorus," I said.

The front door of Merripit House was open. There was no light save in the dining-room, but Holmes caught up the lamp, and left no corner of the house unexplored. No sign could we see of the man whom we were chasing. On the upper floor, however, one of the bedroom doors was locked.

A faint moaning and rustling came from within. Holmes struck the door just over the lock with the flat of his foot, and it flew open. Pistol in hand, we all three rushed into the room.

In the centre of this room there was an upright beam. To this post a figure was tied. In a minute we had torn off the gag, unswathed the bonds, and Mrs Stapleton sank upon the floor in front of us.

"Sir Henry? Is he safe?"

"Yes."

"And the hound?"

"It is dead."

"Thank God! Oh, this villain! See how he has treated me!" She shot her arms out from her sleeves, and we saw with horror that they were all mottled with bruises.

"You bear him no good-will, madam," said Holmes. "Tell us, then, where we shall find him."

"There is but one place where he can have fled," she answered. "There is an old tin mine in the heart of the Mire. It was there that he kept his hound, and there also he had made a refuge."

All pursuit was in vain until the fog had lifted. Meanwhile we left Lestrade at the house, while Holmes and I went back with the baronet to Baskerville Hall.

On the morning after the death of the hound we were guided by Mrs Stapleton through the bog. From amid a tuft of cotton-grass some dark thing was projecting. Holmes seized it, and held an old black boot in the air. 'Meyers, Toronto' was printed on the leather inside.

"It is our friend Sir Henry's missing boot."

"Thrown there by Stapleton in his flight."

"Exactly. He retained it in his hand after using it to set the hound upon his track. He fled still clutching it. And he hurled it away at this point of his flight."

But more than that we were never destined to know, though there was much which we might surmise. If the earth told a true story, then Stapleton never reached that refuge upon that last night. Somewhere in the heart of the Grimpen Mire, this cold and cruel-hearted man is for ever buried.

A Retrospection

It was the end of November, and Holmes and I sat in our sitting-room in Baker Street. I was able to induce him to discuss the details of the

Baskerville mystery.

"My inquiries show that this fellow was indeed a Baskerville. He was a son of that Rodger Baskerville who fled with a sinister reputation to South America. He did marry, and had one child, this fellow. He married Beryl Garçia, changed his name to Vandeleur and fled to England, where he established a school in the east of Yorkshire. The school sank from disrepute into infamy. The Vandeleurs changed their name to Stapleton, and came to the south of England.

"His first act was to establish himself as near to his ancestral home as he could, and to cultivate a friendship with Sir Charles Baskerville.

"Stapleton knew that the old man's heart was weak, and that a shock would kill him. He had heard also that Sir Charles was superstitious, and had taken this grim legend very seriously.

"Having conceived the idea, he proceeded to carry it out with considerable finesse. An ordinary schemer would have been content to work with a savage hound. The use of artificial means to make the creature diabolical was a flash of genius upon his part. He had already learned to penetrate the Grimpen Mire. Here he kennelled it and waited his chance.

"But it was some time coming.

"He found a way out of his difficulties through the chance that Sir Charles made him the minister of his charity in the case of Mrs Laura Lyons. He acquired complete influence over her. He put pressure upon Mrs Lyons to write this letter, prevented her from going, and so had the chance for which he had waited.

"Driving back in the evening from Coombe Tracey, he was in time to get his hound, to treat it with his infernal paint, and to bring the beast to the gate. The dog, incited by its master, sprang over the wicket-gate and pursued the baronet, who fled screaming down the Yew Alley. In that gloomy tunnel it must indeed have been a dreadful sight to see that huge black creature, with its flaming jaws and blazing eyes, bounding after its victim. He fell dead at the end of the alley from heart disease and terror.

"So much for the death of Sir Charles Baskerville. Both of the women concerned in the case, Mrs Stapleton and Mrs Laura Lyons, were left with a strong suspicion against Stapleton. However, both of them were under his influence, and he had nothing to fear from them.

"Stapleton's first idea was that this young stranger from Canada might be done to death in London without coming down to Devonshire at all. His wife had some inkling of his plans; but she dare not write to warn the man she knew to be in danger. Eventually she adopted the expedient of cutting out the words which would form the message, and addressing the letter in a disguised hand.

"It was essential for Stapleton to get some article of Sir Henry's attire to give his scent to the dog. By chance, the first boot which was procured for him was a new one, and, therefore, useless for his purpose. He then obtained another – a most instructive incident, since it proved that we were dealing with a real hound.

"The Stapletons then went down to Devonshire, whither they were soon followed by Sir Henry and you.

"It was my game to watch Stapleton. I could not do this if I were with you, since he would be keenly on his guard. I came down secretly when I was supposed to be in London.

"Your reports were of great service. I was able to establish the identity of the man and the woman.

"By the time that you discovered me upon the moor I had a complete knowledge of the whole business, but I had not a case which could go to a jury. There seemed to be no alternative but to catch him red-handed, and to do so we had to use Sir Henry as a bait. We did so, and we succeeded in completing our case and driving Stapleton to his destruction. And now, my dear Watson, we have had some weeks of severe work, and for one evening, I think, we may turn our thoughts into more pleasant channels. I have a box for *Les Huguenots*. Might I trouble you to be ready in half an hour, and we can stop at Marcini's for a little dinner on the way?"